Splash's
Secret Friend

Dolphin School

Splash's Secret Friend

by Catherine Hapka
illustrated by Hollie Hibbert

SCHOLASTIC INC.

Text copyright © 2015 by Catherine Hapka
Illustrations copyright © 2015 by Scholastic Inc.

ISBN 978-0-545-75026-4

10 9 8 7 6 5 4 3 2   16 17 18 19/0

Printed in the U.S.A.   40
First printing, September 2015
Book design by Jennifer Rinaldi Windau

1

The Shark Migration

"Thanks for swimming me to school again today, Dad," Pearl said.

Her father smiled. "You're welcome, Pearl," he said with a flick of his tail. "I know you're used to swimming to school by yourself. But it's best for all dolphins to be careful during the shark migration."

Pearl shivered and glanced around. The Salty Sea was calm and peaceful. Bright sunlight filtered through the clear water all the way to the shallow, sandy seafloor. Schools of colorful fish darted in and out among the coral, and a jellyfish floated near the surface. Everything looked normal. There were no sharks in sight.

Still, Pearl felt a little bit nervous. It was the time of the annual shark migration, when lots of sharks moved from one area of the Salty Sea to another. Her class had been learning all about it in Ocean Lore.

"Mom told me the sharks don't usually come close to Coral Cove Dolphin School," she said. "I'm glad about that!" Pearl had been nervous about leaving her pod's safe home lagoon, even with her father along. But her mother said the waters in their part of the sea were mostly too shallow for the larger sharks.

"It's just a precaution," Pearl's mother had told her. "Sharks can be unpredictable."

Sharks could be scary, too. Pearl's father had a scar on his fin from a shark attack when he was young. Every time she saw it, Pearl could only think one thing: Stay away from sharks!

She was glad when the familiar school reef came into view. Coral Cove Dolphin School was encircled by a large reef made up of every kind of coral, sea fan, sponge, and algae Pearl could imagine. It was also the home to countless other creatures, from anemones to fish. Pearl always felt safe when she was inside the school reef's colorful walls.

"Be careful swimming back," she told her father.

"I will," he promised. "Be sure your friends swim you home after school, all right?"

When Pearl swam into the cove, her friends Echo and Flip were floating near the entrance. The two of them were members of the same large pod. They usually swam to school together, along with a group of older students from their pod.

"Pearl!" Echo swam over. "Did your dad swim you to school again today?"

"Yes," Pearl said. "He said we're being extra careful until the migration is over." She looked around. "Where's Splash?"

"He's not here yet." Echo sounded a tiny bit worried. "That's weird, right?"

Pearl nodded. Splash was the fastest swimmer in their class. He was usually one of the first dolphins to arrive at school.

"I'm sure he'll be here soon," Flip said. "Anyway, he's fast enough to outswim any dumb old shark." He did a flip in the water. "Just like me!"

At that moment an older student swam past. His name was Mullet, and he was friends with Splash's older brother, Finny. That didn't mean he was friends with Splash and the others, though. He loved to tease and make fun of the younger dolphins whenever the teachers weren't looking.

"What are you babies talking about?" Mullet asked with a smirk. "Let me guess—

your fins are quivering because you're scared of sharks?"

Echo frowned at him. "It's smart to be cautious of sharks," she said. "Even Old Salty says so. He says that if we see a shark, we should swim fast in the other direction."

Old Salty was the principal of the school. He also taught Ocean Lore. He knew just about everything about all the creatures under the sea.

"It's smart for babies like you to be cautious," Mullet said. "If you saw a shark up close, you'd probably—"

He stopped talking suddenly. Pearl soon figured out why. One of the teachers, Bay, was swimming toward them.

Bay was Pearl's favorite teacher, and she taught her two favorite classes—Magic and Music. "It's almost time for school to begin,"

Bay told Pearl and her friends. "Mullet, shouldn't you be heading to class, too?"

"Yes, Bay," Mullet said sweetly. "I was just leaving."

"He's such a sneak!" Echo whispered to Pearl. "He always acts nice in front of the teachers."

Pearl just nodded. She wasn't really thinking about Mullet anymore. "I wonder where Splash could be," she said. "He's still not here."

"I hope he didn't run into some migrating sharks," Flip said.

"Don't say that!" Echo exclaimed. "He'll probably be here any second now."

But Splash still hadn't arrived when Music class started. Pearl kept looking toward the school entrance, but there was no sign of him.

Bay told the class that they would be working on a magic-strengthening song today. All dolphins had natural magical abilities, and when they sang, it made their magic stronger.

"Why don't you start, Wiggle?" Bay said to one of the boys. "Sing the first section of the song we learned yesterday, and then the dolphin next to you can sing the next part. We'll go around the circle like that."

"Okay." Wiggle was a small dolphin with a pointy snout. He hardly ever stayed still for more than a second. He darted up to the surface to take a breath, then settled himself back in his spot with a wiggle of his fins.

Then he started singing. After a moment, the girl next to him took over.

Meanwhile, Pearl looked over at the

entrance again. Where could Splash be?

She got distracted from her worries when Flip started to sing right next to her. He was loud but kept messing up the tune.

There was a flash of movement over near the entrance. Pearl looked that way, hoping it was Splash. But it was only a colorful angelfish swimming by.

"Pearl? Pearl!" Bay's voice broke into her thoughts. "It's your turn."

"Oops!" Pearl quickly turned back. "Sorry. Um, where were we?"

Flip sang the last line again. Pearl nodded and sang her part.

But as soon as she finished and Echo took over, Pearl went right back to worrying about Splash. What if he'd run into something unexpected on his way to school—like a hungry shark?

2
Echo's Idea

"I'm here! I'm here!" Splash burst into the cove with a swirl of bubbles. "Sorry I'm late."

"Splash!" Pearl cried with relief. "Where were you?"

Splash was swimming so fast that he bumped into Flip before he could stop. "Sorry," he told him.

"What kept you, Splash?" Bay asked. "Class started several minutes ago."

"I know. I'm sorry." Splash swam up to gulp

in air through his blowhole. "I hope I didn't interrupt."

"You did," Flip told him. "But that's okay. Echo was messing up her part, anyway."

"I was not!" Echo protested.

Bay ignored both of them. "Please answer my question, Splash," she said. "Why are you late?"

Splash looked around. "It was nothing, really," he said. "Um, just one of those things, you know . . ."

Pearl traded a surprised look with Echo. Splash wasn't acting like himself. Normally he was cheerful and straightforward. When someone asked him a question, he gave an honest answer. Right now it seemed as if he didn't want to answer Bay at all.

"I know!" Wiggle exclaimed, wiggling his flukes. "I bet you ran into some migrating sharks, didn't you?"

"You shouldn't be ashamed to admit it if that's why you're late," Echo told Splash. "Any of us would hide if we saw a shark, too."

"No!" Splash said quickly. "That's definitely not it. I haven't been anywhere near any sharks. Old Salty told us to stay far away from sharks, remember?" He looked at Bay. "I just, um, stopped to watch some shrimp that were arguing over some food. I guess I forgot about the time."

"I see." Bay nodded, seeming satisfied with the answer. "All right, then. Please don't let it happen again."

"Okay." Splash took his place beside Echo.

As class resumed, Pearl couldn't help peeking past Echo at Splash. It wasn't hard to believe he might have stopped to watch some shrimp. But if that was why he was late, why hadn't he said so right away? Why had he acted so oddly?

Oh well, she thought. *I'm sure he'll tell us at recess. I'm just glad he didn't run into a hungry shark after all!*

After Music came Jumping and Swimming class. The teacher, Riptide, was big and burly and loud. He liked to get started right away and keep the class moving the whole time. Pearl was too busy trying to keep up to wonder about Splash's behavior.

After Jumping and Swimming came recess. Pearl, Echo, and Flip gathered around Splash. "So why were you really late today?" Echo asked.

"What do you mean?" Splash said. "I already told you. I got distracted by some shrimp. Now come on, who wants to play hide-and-seek?"

"Maybe later," Flip said. "Are you sure the shrimp thing is the real reason?"

Splash did a flip in the water. "What else would it be? Okay, who wants to be it?"

Pearl felt worried. Splash was still behaving strangely!

Echo and Flip looked worried, too. "Splash, you've been acting weird all day," Echo said. "You didn't even win any of the races in Jumping and Swimming today!"

Pearl realized she was right. That *was* weird—Splash almost always came in first in all the races and contests in Jumping and Swimming. Could he be sick?

"You can tell us if something's wrong," she told him. "We're your friends. We want to help."

"I don't know what you're talking about," Splash said. "There's nothing wrong. Anyway, I can't talk any more right now. I forgot—I need to ask my brother something. I think I see him over near the entrance."

He flicked his flukes, swimming off at a fast pace before anyone else could say anything.

Echo stared after him. "That was weird," she said. "Splash isn't a liar. But I don't think he was telling us the truth just now, do you?"

Pearl shook her head. "I wish we knew why," she said quietly.

"Me too," Flip said. "Let's ask him again after he finishes talking to his brother."

But Splash didn't return. Even when recess ended, Pearl didn't see him anywhere. She swam with the others to the area of the cove where they always went for Ocean Lore class. Old Salty was already there chatting with some of the other students. But there was no sign of Splash.

"I hope he's not late for this class, too,"

Pearl whispered to Echo. "Old Salty doesn't like it when we're late."

"I know," Echo said. Then she looked past Pearl and smiled. "Oh, good. Here he comes."

Splash swam over just as Old Salty called for attention. That meant Pearl and the others didn't get a chance to talk to him.

"All right, young students," Old Salty said in his deep, crusty voice. "We've been talking about sharks for several days now, and I'm sure you're all getting a little tired of the topic."

One of the other girls giggled quietly. Pearl was pretty sure she knew why. Old Salty was nice, but his lectures were almost always boring!

The teacher didn't hear the giggle. "So now," he said, "we'll move on to something more interesting: algae!"

Echo groaned softly. "Algae again?" she whispered.

But Pearl didn't care how boring Old Salty's lecture was today. She was still thinking about Splash.

What in the sea could be going on with her friend?

3

Splash's Surprise

When school ended for the day, Splash dashed out of the cove at top speed. "Hey, wait up!" Flip yelled, swimming after him.

Pearl and Echo followed. They all caught up to Splash outside.

"What's the matter with you, anyway?" Flip said, sounding annoyed. "You're acting like a real barnacle-head today!"

"No, I'm not," Splash said. "I'm just in a hurry to get home, that's all."

"You mean because of the shark migration?" Echo asked. "I don't blame you for being worried about that."

"Yeah." Pearl shivered. "I'm glad the migration will be over soon!"

"It doesn't have anything to do with sharks," Splash said. "I already told you that."

"Aha!" Flip said. "You just admitted there's something wrong."

"No, I didn't," Splash said. "There's nothing wrong."

"Then why did you say 'It doesn't have anything to do with sharks'?" Flip said. "That's admitting there's something wrong—just not sharks, right?"

Splash's fins drooped. "Okay, you caught me." He blew bubbles out of his blowhole in a big sigh. "Anyway, I hate trying to keep a secret from my best friends."

"A secret?" Echo said. "What kind of secret?"

Splash looked around, then swam closer and lowered his voice. "If I tell you, do you promise you won't be upset?"

Pearl looked at the others. What kind of secret would upset them? Wondering made her feel a little nervous.

"We promise," Echo said after a moment. "Right, guys?"

"Sure, I promise," Pearl said.

"Me too," Flip added. "Now what's your big secret, Splash?"

"I'll show you," Splash said. "But you have to promise one more thing. You can't tell anyone else, no matter what. Nobody. I mean it."

"Okay," Flip said right away.

But this time Echo hesitated even longer, looking uneasy. Pearl knew how she felt, since she didn't really like the thought of making that kind of promise. She was used to telling her parents everything. She didn't want to keep any secrets from her teachers, either.

"Do you promise?" Splash asked the two girls.

Finally Echo nodded. "I promise," she said in a quiet voice.

"I do, too," Pearl said. Splash was their friend. She knew he wouldn't ask them to keep a secret unless it was something really important.

"Good." Splash sounded a little happier. "Then come with me."

He swam off away from the school reef. His friends followed.

"We're not going to Bigsky Basin, are we?" Flip asked.

He sounded nervous, and Pearl could guess why. On the first day of school, Mullet had dared Flip to swim out into the deeper water of the Basin all by himself. He'd run into a huge tiger shark out there, and had barely escaped. Pearl still felt scared when she thought about it. She wondered if any sharks were migrating through Bigsky Basin right at that moment.

Either way, she was glad when Splash said they weren't going anywhere near there.

"So where are we going?" Echo asked, flicking her flukes to catch up with Splash.

"You'll see." Splash glanced behind him. "Nobody saw us swim this way, did they?"

"I don't think so," Pearl said. "But aren't you going to tell us where you're taking us?"

"To meet a new friend," Splash said.

"A new friend?" Flip said. "What do you mean? Another dolphin?"

"No," Splash said. "Please don't ask any more questions, okay? You should wait and see for yourselves."

"Okay," Pearl said. She tried to imagine what kind of friend Splash meant. If it wasn't a dolphin, it had to be some other kind of sea creature. But why would Splash think they'd be upset if he'd made friends with a lobster or a manta ray or something? Pearl had befriended several of the sea turtles who lived in her home lagoon. Her little sister, Squeak, was good friends with a reef squid who lived there, too.

Splash was swimming even faster now, so Pearl had to work hard to keep up. When they neared a large clump of stony coral, he stopped suddenly.

"We're almost there," he said, sounding nervous. "Don't forget your promise, okay?"

"We won't," Echo said. "Now where's this new friend of yours?"

"Is that him over there?" Flip swam toward a passing puffer fish. But the fish ignored him and kept swimming. "Oh. I guess not."

Pearl looked around. There weren't many

fish or other sea creatures nearby. The only ones she saw were an eel and a couple of sea urchins. Was one of those creatures Splash's new friend?

"Okay." Splash blew out a stream of bubbles. "Are you guys ready to meet him now?"

"Hold on, I'm almost out of air," Echo said. She swam up to the surface and sucked in a breath. Pearl and Flip did the same.

So did Splash. Only instead of stopping right at the surface, he kept going. He burst out of the water and did an unusual spinning leap.

When he splashed back down again, Flip looked impressed. "Hey, where'd you learn to do that jump?" he exclaimed. "You've got to teach me—I bet even Riptide would be impressed if we showed him that move!"

"Just come on," Splash said without answering him. "It's this way."

He darted off, swimming around the coral. The others followed. Once again, Pearl had to swim as fast as she could to keep up.

But when she rounded the coral, she stopped short. Splash was just ahead—snout to snout with a shark!

4
Spinner

"Look out, Splash!" Flip shouted.

"We'll save you!" Echo added. "Come on, guys—let's join our magic."

She stuck out her fin. Pearl touched it with her own, focusing her magic energy. Echo was the best of anyone in their class at magic. Maybe she could stop the shark long enough for Splash to get out of range of its sharp teeth.

"Wait!" Splash yelled.

Their magic was already flowing out toward the shark. Pearl could tell that Echo was trying to immobilize the creature with a type of magic called *pushing*. Dolphins didn't like to use pushing unless they had no other choice, since it forced other creatures to do something they didn't want to do. But this was an emergency!

"You guys, stop!" Splash exclaimed. He swam right into the flow of energy, blocking it.

"Get out of the way!" Flip cried. "That shark is small—we can totally get away before he tries to bite you."

"He's not going to bite me," Splash insisted.

"Yeah," the shark said. "I'm not going to bite him. I might bite *you* if you don't stop throwing your goofy dolphin magic at me, though!"

Splash frowned at the shark. "Quiet, Spinner. You're not helping."

Echo's eyes went wide. "You know his name?" She was so surprised, her magic stopped.

Pearl was surprised, too. "What's going on?" she exclaimed.

"That's what I'm trying to tell you." Splash blew out a frustrated stream of bubbles. "This is the friend I was telling you about. His name is Spinner."

All three of Splash's friends stared at the shark. He was a blacktip, one of the smaller shark species in the Salty Sea. Pearl could tell he was young—probably around their age.

"Hi," Spinner said. Then he turned to Splash and bared his teeth. "I thought you weren't going to tell anyone I was here."

"I know," Splash replied. "But you don't have to worry. These are my friends—the ones I was telling you about yesterday."

Spinner's small black eyes swept over Pearl and the others. Pearl shivered, looking at his teeth.

"What's going on, Splash?" Echo sounded brave, but Pearl could see her fins shaking. "Why are you hanging out with this . . . this . . . *shark*?"

"Spinner needs help," Splash said. "He was migrating through Bigsky Basin when he got separated from his pod."

"Sharks don't live in pods," Spinner broke in. "That's a dolphin thing. We live in schools."

"Okay," Splash said. "Anyway, you got separated from your family, right?"

"Right." Spinner was swimming around behind Splash, his tail flicking with each turn. "Then a big, mean bull shark chased me, and I ended up stuck in a hole in some coral."

Splash looked at his friends. "That's where I found him," he said. "I heard him thrashing on my way home from school yesterday."

"He saved me." Spinner stopped swimming and stared at Splash. "I never expected that from a dolphin."

Splash smiled at him. "It's our job," he said. "Dolphins are the protectors of the ocean."

Pearl nodded. She'd heard that all her life. But normally dolphins had to protect other creatures from sharks—not protect the sharks themselves!

"Anyway, I helped him get out of the coral, and then found him a better place to hide until we figure out how he can get back to his family," Splash said.

Spinner was swimming again. This time he started moving in a large circle around the whole group. Pearl felt nervous when he passed behind her. He wasn't very big, and Splash said he was his friend. But he was still a shark!

Echo looked nervous, too. "What are you doing back there?" she said. "Stop circling us like that."

"Why?" Spinner kept swimming.

"Because!" Echo cried. She tried to dart out of the circle before Spinner came around again.

But the shark put on a sudden burst of speed, blocking her way. "Where are you going?" he demanded.

Echo's fins were shaking again. But her voice was steady as she responded. "I'm swimming straight back to school," she announced, looking Spinner square in the eye. "I'm going to tell the teachers there's a shark hiding out in our reef!"

5

Deciding
What to Do

"You're *not* telling anyone about me!"
Spinner said. He bared his teeth, then bumped
Echo with his snout, forcing her back over
with the others.

"Stop it!" Echo shouted. "You'd better stop,
or . . . or . . ."

"Or what?" Spinner sneered. "You'll attack
me with magical dancing lights?"

"Stop it, everyone!" Splash exclaimed.

"Look, Spinner, you're scaring them. They aren't used to being around sharks."

He swam over and shoved Spinner with his head, pushing him away from the other dolphins. Pearl held her breath, terrified that the shark would bite her friend. She was relieved when Spinner grumbled, but didn't fight back.

"That's right," Flip said, flapping his fins. "You'd better stay away from us, shark face!"

"Fine," Spinner muttered, swimming back and forth behind Splash, who stayed between him and the others. "I forgot that most dolphins are kind of wimpy. Anyway, I wasn't trying to scare you." He glared at Echo with his shiny black eyes. "I just didn't want you to leave."

Echo frowned at him. "Try asking me nicely next time. That works better."

"Okay," Splash said. "Now listen, Echo. You can't tell the teachers, or anyone else, that Spinner is here."

"Why not?" Echo still sounded upset. "Old Salty told us to stay far away from all sharks."

"Exactly. He'll be mad if he knows I helped one." Splash glanced at Spinner. "Plus, he'll probably chase Spinner away from the reef."

"So what if he does?" Flip blew out a noisy stream of bubbles. "Sharks never help dolphins! I say we chase him off the reef ourselves!"

"Oh yeah?" Spinner bared his teeth. "I'd like to see you try."

"I still think we should get the teachers," Echo put in.

"Stop!" Splash sounded upset. "All of you—stop fighting! Do you really want to chase Spinner away? What do you think will happen to him out there all alone?"

"I'll tell you what," Spinner said darkly. "I'll become some oversized tiger shark or great white's dinner. That's what."

Pearl shuddered. Spinner was kind of prickly and different. But she didn't want him to become another shark's dinner!

She stared at Spinner, trying to imagine how he felt. It wasn't easy. Sharks were very different from dolphins! But in Pearl's home lagoon, her pod helped baby sea turtles find their way out to sea. That meant Pearl was used to trying to see the world through the eyes of a different species.

Sharks were much scarier than turtles. But

any creature would be scared and lonely being away from his family.

"Splash might be right," she spoke up. "Maybe we should help Spinner."

"What?" Flip cried. Echo didn't say anything, but she looked surprised.

Pearl turned to Spinner. "You said you live in a school," she said. "And that it's like a dolphin pod?"

"I guess so," Spinner said. "I live with a bunch of other young sharks, and a few adults, too."

"Okay, so you live in a school," Flip said. "Do you go to school, too? Like we do?" He still sounded suspicious of Spinner. But now he sounded curious, too.

Spinner nodded. "At Shark Academy we learn all about hunting, and shark history, and stuff like that." He looked sad for a minute. "I miss my best friends, Toothy and Dora."

Pearl looked at her own best friends. "He's really not so different from us after all," she told them. "We have to help him, the same way my pod helps the sea turtles."

"But sea turtles are nice," Echo protested. "Sharks are mean!"

"I'm not mean." Spinner bared his teeth at her. "I'm just not a wimp, like dolphins." Then he shot a look at Splash. "Most dolphins, I mean. Some are okay."

"Every creature in the sea has its place," Pearl reminded Echo. "Even sharks."

"Yeah. Sharks are the best!" Spinner did a spinning underwater flip.

"Hey, that looked like the flip Splash did earlier," Flip said. "Did you teach him that, Spinner?"

"Yes, he did," Splash said. "If you help him, maybe he'll teach you, too."

Flip still didn't look too sure. But finally he nodded. "I guess Pearl is right. We're supposed to protect all sea creatures." He looked at Spinner. "That includes sharks."

Splash smiled with relief. "Echo? What about you?"

Echo looked nervous. But she nodded, too. "Okay," she said quietly. "Let's help him find his family."

"Thanks." Spinner bared his teeth at all of them. It took Pearl a moment to realize he was smiling.

Just then all of them heard someone swimming their way. Flip peered around the coral formation.

"Quiet, everyone!" he whispered. "It's Mullet!"

"Oh no," Echo muttered. "What's he doing here?"

"Who's Mullet?" Spinner asked.

"Another dolphin," Splash whispered. "Not a nice one, though. He's always picking on us."

"Really?" Spinner peeked out as Mullet swam past. "Don't worry. He didn't even look this way."

"Good," Splash said. "Let's give him a few minutes to get farther away. Then we should go."

"What?" Spinner sounded dismayed. "But

we haven't decided how I'm going to get home!"

Splash touched Spinner's fin with his own. "I know, but it's getting late. Don't worry. We'll be back tomorrow morning to figure out a plan."

6
Morning Meeting

"I'M GLAD YOU'RE SO EAGER TO GET TO SCHOOL this morning, Pearl," Pearl's father said with a chuckle. "But slow down—your old dad is having trouble keeping up with you!"

Pearl smiled and slowed down. But not too much. She'd asked her father to swim her to school early. He hadn't asked why, which was a relief. She'd promised Splash that she wouldn't tell anyone about Spinner, but she didn't like the thought of lying to her parents.

"How long until the shark migration is over?" she asked as they continued on their way, skirting the edge of Bigsky Basin. Being so close to the deep water always made Pearl a little nervous—especially now.

"A few more days," her father replied. "Then everything can go back to normal."

"Good. I'm glad most of the sharks will be away from here soon." Pearl hesitated. "I bet you are, too. You must hate sharks a whole lot, huh?"

Her father looked surprised. "Of course I don't," he said. "I don't hate any sea creature."

"But your fin . . ." Pearl waved a flipper at the scar on his dorsal fin. "A shark attacked you!"

He chuckled. "Yes. That was just a shark being a shark."

"Okay." Pearl felt confused. "But it probably would have eaten you if your pod hadn't rescued you in time, right?"

"Probably," her father agreed.

Pearl shook her head. "So why don't you hate sharks after that?"

"Hating all sharks for the actions of one would be foolish," her father said. "Besides, hating a shark for wanting to eat would be like hating a seagull for wanting to fly."

"Oh." Pearl had never thought about it that way. "Okay. But adults are always telling us to stay far away from sharks."

"Yes. That's because we respect the danger some of the larger sharks can pose to dolphins. It's why I'm swimming you to school during the migration. But that doesn't mean we hate or fear all sharks." He touched her fin with his own. "And I hope you don't, either, Pearl. Sharks are not our enemies. Dolphins don't believe in enemies."

"I don't hate them," she said softly, thinking about Spinner.

"Good." Her father chuckled. "Of course, that doesn't mean you should invite a shark home to the lagoon to visit or anything!"

Pearl forced a smile. But secretly she felt worried. Her father might not hate sharks like she'd thought. Still, it sounded as if he believed she should stay away from them. What would he think if he knew about Spinner?

She felt confused and a little guilty at the thought of keeping such an important secret from him. But in a way, her talk with her father had also made her feel better about the plan to help Spinner. Her parents believed in helping all creatures, so it was probably what they would do themselves. Pearl only wished she could tell them the truth so they could help figure out a plan.

But she couldn't tell anyone. She'd made a promise to Splash. A true friend would never break a promise, and Pearl wanted to be a good friend.

Echo, Splash, and Flip were waiting outside the school reef. "Well, look at this!" Pearl's father said with a smile. "It looks like everyone is eager to get to school this morning."

"Yes," Echo spoke up with a smile. "We love school. Right, Pearl?"

"Right. Okay, thanks for swimming me here, Dad." Pearl rubbed his fin quickly. "See you later."

"Bye, kids," he said. "Pay attention to your teachers and learn a lot today, okay?"

As soon as he swam away, Pearl and her friends hurried in the opposite direction, toward Spinner's hiding place. "I thought you'd never get here, Pearl," Flip complained. "We'll have to hurry to figure out a plan and get back in time for Music class."

"Less talking, more swimming," Echo told him. "The sooner we get there, the sooner we can get back."

Splash was out ahead of the others. He was the first to round the coral formation. "Hey, Spinner," he called. "Come out here. We don't have much time."

There was no response. "Spinner?" Pearl said, swimming forward beside Splash. "Where is he?"

"I don't know." Splash frowned. "He's not in the hiding place, or—"

"Listen," Echo interrupted. "I can hear something over that way."

She was looking toward a wall of coral a short distance away. Now Pearl heard the commotion, too. It sounded like someone swimming and yelling over there on the other side of the coral.

"Let's see what's going on," Splash said, sounding worried.

They all swam toward the wall. When they rounded the edge of it, Pearl gasped.

Spinner was there, jaws open in a toothy snarl as he chased a terrified Mullet!

7

The Chase

"Spinner, stop!" Splash cried. "What are you doing?"

Spinner was pretty far ahead of them, and Mullet was even farther ahead. At first Pearl wasn't sure either of them could hear Splash.

Then Splash called out again, and Spinner stopped and turned around. Mullet kept going, though. He didn't slow down until he was completely out of sight.

"Wow," Flip said. "I never saw Mullet swim so fast."

Pearl nodded. "I don't think he even knew

we were here," she said. "That's good, since he'd probably tattle on us to the teachers."

Spinner was swimming toward them, grinning. "Did you see that dolphin go?" he called. "He was so scared he practically left his fins behind!"

"I can't believe you did that!" Splash sounded upset. "Now you've really done it, Spinner!"

Spinner looked surprised. "What do you mean? I was just trying to be a good friend."

"A good friend?" Echo exclaimed. "By trying to eat our classmate?"

"You said that dolphin picks on you all the time." Spinner frowned. "That makes him your enemy, right? When I saw him swimming past my hiding place, I figured I'd pay you back for helping me by giving him a good scare."

Pearl could tell that the young shark was honestly confused. Had he really thought he was being nice by chasing Mullet?

Maybe he did, she thought. *That just goes to show how different dolphins and sharks really are.*

"Dolphins don't have enemies," she told Spinner, remembering what her father had said just a little while ago. "Especially not other dolphins."

"Yeah. Anyway, you can't do stuff like that," Echo exclaimed, glaring at Spinner. "You could have gotten Splash—and the rest of us—in big trouble!"

"Exactly," Flip added. "It's just lucky that Mullet didn't see us." He glanced off in the direction Mullet had gone. "Probably."

"He definitely saw Spinner, though." Splash

still sounded upset. "He's probably on his way back to school right now to tell the teachers there's a shark in the area."

Pearl hadn't thought of that. "Oh no. What are we going to do?"

Flip shrugged. "What *can* we do?" he said. "Sorry, Spinner. We tried to help, but you messed it up. Now you'll have to take your chances getting home on your own, unless you want to hang around and wait for the adult dolphins to chase you off, that is."

"No!" Splash cried. "We can't just give up."

"Why not?" Echo said, still frowning.

"Because Spinner's our friend," Splash insisted. "We have to help him. Right, Pearl?"

Pearl hesitated, looking at Spinner. She wanted to help him, but he was making it so difficult! Maybe it would be better to let the teachers find him. Then they could decide what to do with him.

Spinner stared at her. "I'm sorry," he said. "I was trying to be nice. I promise."

That made Pearl change her mind. "It's okay," she told Spinner. Then she looked at her friends. "Splash is right—we have to try to help him. He's our friend. That's the right thing to do."

At least I think *it is*, she added to herself.

Echo and Flip still looked uncertain. But they both nodded.

"All right," Echo said. "If you say so, Pearl."

"Good." Splash sounded relieved. "Hurry, we need to find him a new hiding place before Mullet comes back here with the teachers."

They split up and swam around. Finally Flip

found a cave in some coral a good distance away.

"Perfect," Splash said as Spinner swam into the cave. He was completely hidden from view behind some waving sea plumes in front of the entrance. "You can hide in here whenever you hear someone coming. We'll come back after school."

After that, the four dolphin friends had to hurry to make it back to Coral Cove Dolphin School. They swam in through the entrance just as it was time for classes to begin.

"Do you see Mullet anywhere?" Splash whispered as they swam toward the Music area. Bay was talking to Old Salty over near the kelp forest, so the friends had a moment to talk.

Echo looked around. "He's over there with Finny and Shelly and the rest of his school pod," she whispered back. "I guess he didn't tell the teachers what happened after all."

"Why not?" Flip wondered. "That's kind of weird."

For a second Pearl was ready to agree. Then she thought about it and realized that maybe it wasn't so weird after all.

"Not really," she said. "He was probably too embarrassed to tell anyone he was scared of such a small shark."

Echo nodded. "You're probably right. Plus, blacktip sharks don't usually eat dolphins. They're too small."

"Yeah." Flip grinned. "We should remind him of that next time he calls us scaredy-babies."

"No!" Splash warned. "You can't say anything to him about Spinner. Not until we get him back to his family."

"Not after that, either," Echo said. "If he knows we were helping a shark, he'd tell the teachers for sure. We'd be in big trouble."

"Oh, right." Flip nodded. "Okay, I won't say a word."

"Good." Pearl shot another uneasy glance at Mullet. "We'll just have to hope that Mullet doesn't say a word about Spinner, either."

8
Magic and Mullet

THE SCHOOL DAY SEEMED TO GO ON FOREVER, at least to Pearl. Finally it was time for Magic, the last class of the day.

"All right, students," Bay said. "Today we're going to begin learning some of the basics of physical magic."

Pearl had been worrying about Spinner and Mullet all day. But Bay's words made her forget about all that for a moment. So far, the young dolphins had been practicing only mental magic. That included skills like guiding and pushing, along with mental messaging. On the first day of school, Bay had promised that they'd be learning about physical magic, too.

"Will we start with healing?" one of the other students, Harmony, asked eagerly. "I saw some dolphins from my pod heal an injured whale once."

"We'll get to healing soon." Bay nodded at Harmony. "But we're going to start with something a bit easier."

"Good," Splash said. "The easier the better!"

That made everyone laugh, including Bay. They all knew that Splash did a lot better in Jumping and Swimming class than he did in Magic.

"Don't be down on yourself, Splash," the teacher said with a smile. "Your magic is getting better all the time."

"That's true," Echo told him. "Just yesterday

you guided that crab all the way around in a circle, remember?"

Splash laughed again. "Only because Pearl was adding her magic to mine."

"That's important for everyone," Bay reminded him. "All dolphin magic works best when we work together. That will be especially important for today's exercise. We're going to learn how to use physical magic to make sounds louder or softer."

Pearl had seen her parents use that kind of magic many times. They often made their voices louder when they sang to the baby sea turtles in their lagoon.

She listened as Bay talked about what to do. But after a moment, Pearl's thoughts drifted back to Spinner. What was the shark doing right now? Was he scared out there all alone?

She also couldn't stop worrying about Mullet. What if he decided to tell someone he'd been chased by a shark? The teachers wouldn't want a shark so close to the school. They'd probably go out there, find Spinner, and chase him far, far away . . .

Pearl had to stop thinking about that when Bay told them it was time to practice what they'd just learned. Pearl and Flip were partners for the exercise. They were supposed to sing a few notes and try to make the sound louder.

The first time they tried, Pearl sang a little bit of the song they'd learned in Music two days earlier. Flip touched her fin, and the two of them focused their magic just like Bay had told them. The notes rang out across the lagoon, much louder than Pearl was really singing.

"Well done," Bay said. "That was very good for your first try. Next?"

She turned to Wiggle and his partner, Harmony. Pearl tried to pay attention, but it wasn't easy. Soon she was back to thinking about Mullet and Spinner.

She was still thinking about them when her team's turn came around again. "I'll sing this time," Flip offered.

He sang out a few notes and held out his fin toward Pearl. But she didn't notice. She was too busy trying to figure out a way to help Spinner. They needed to hurry—the more time that passed, the harder it would be for him to catch up to his family.

Meanwhile, Flip was sending out magic energy. The notes he was singing came out a tiny bit louder than normal. But the song wasn't nearly as loud as their first try.

"Hey," Flip complained. "Pearl, you need to help!"

"Oops." Pearl finally noticed what was going on. She reached for Flip's fin, but it was too late. He'd stopped singing.

"Pearl, are you all right?" Bay asked. "I can tell you're not as focused as usual today."

"Sorry." Pearl felt embarrassed. "May we try it again?"

"Of course." Bay swam a little closer and peered at her. "But is anything wrong? It's not like you to be so distracted."

"I know. I'm sorry." Pearl smiled, hoping the teacher wouldn't ask any more questions. There *was* something wrong: Pearl was worried about Spinner. But she couldn't tell Bay about that. Not after the promise she'd made to Splash.

Luckily, Bay just nodded and told Pearl and Flip to try again. This time, they did much better.

Pearl was relieved when class finally ended. She started to swim off with her friends. But Bay called her name.

"Could I talk to you for a moment?" the teacher asked.

"Of course." Pearl looked at her friends. "I'll meet you guys by the exit."

When the others were gone, Bay looked serious. "I just want to make sure everything is all right," she said. "You were very quiet in both of my classes today. Are you nervous about the shark migration?"

"No," Pearl said quickly. That much was true. She'd been so busy worrying about Spinner that she'd almost forgotten to worry about other sharks.

Bay waited, as if expecting Pearl to say more. When she didn't, the teacher blew out a bubbly sigh.

"I don't mean to pry, Pearl," she said. "You're one of my best students, and I worry when a good student seems to be having trouble."

"I know." Pearl felt terrible. Bay looked so concerned! "The truth is, I *am* worried about something. But I promised someone I wouldn't say anything about it. I . . . I don't want to break my promise."

"I see." Bay looked troubled, but she nodded. "In that case, I'll stop asking questions. I'd never ask you to betray a friend's secret. But I hope you know that you can come to me—or any of the other teachers—if you should ever need help."

"I know," Pearl said. "Thanks."

When she joined her friends, they all looked worried. "What did Bay want?" Echo asked.

"She could tell that something was upsetting me," Pearl replied. "But don't worry, I didn't tell her about Spinner."

"Good." Splash was already moving. "Let's go."

They swam toward the exit. "Look out," Echo whispered. "There's Mullet."

The older student was drifting in the quiet water just inside the entryway. Pearl hoped he didn't notice them going by and decide to tease them.

When they passed, he swam forward. "Hey," he said. "Have you guys seen Finny or Shelly?"

"No," Echo said. "Sorry."

"Oh." Mullet frowned. Pearl waited for him to say something else. But he just turned and looked around.

"That was weird," Flip said once the four friends were outside. "I thought Mullet would say something mean for sure."

"Me too," Splash agreed. "Maybe getting chased by Spinner spooked him out of being such a bully."

"I doubt it," Pearl said. "But maybe it scared

him enough that he doesn't want to swim out of school alone."

"Mullet? Scared?" Flip sounded surprised. "Wow."

Pearl knew how he felt. Mullet always acted as if nothing scared him.

"Even if he's nervous now, it probably won't last," Echo predicted. "We need to figure out a plan to help Spinner before Mullet decides to tell someone what happened."

"You're right." Splash flicked his tail and shot off. "Let's go!"

9
Pearl's Plan

SPINNER CAME OUT OF HIS HIDING CAVE AS soon as the friends arrived. "I thought you'd never get here," he complained. "Dolphins are so slow!"

Pearl ignored that. "We need to come up with a plan right away," she told the young shark. "Mullet hasn't told anyone about you yet. But we're worried that he might."

"So let's start thinking of plans," Splash said. "Who has an idea?"

"I do!" Flip spurted some bubbles out of his blowhole. "We could disguise Spinner as a dolphin. Then we could swim him right past everyone."

Echo stared at him. "Disguise him as a dolphin? How are we supposed to do that—pull out all his teeth?"

"No way!" Spinner said. "I like my teeth right where they are." He bared them in a snarl.

Pearl shuddered. She didn't like looking at those sharp teeth!

"Sorry, Flip," she said. "I don't think we can disguise him well enough to fool anyone. Any other ideas?"

"We don't even know where his family is right now," Echo said. "Maybe we need to work on that first. Otherwise, sneaking him out of the cove won't make any difference."

"Okay," Splash said. "How can we find them?"

"Maybe we could get a seagull to look," Flip suggested.

Echo looked dubious. "Seagulls don't think about anything except food," she said. "How could we convince one to help us?"

"We could give it some food," Flip said. "Then it would want to help."

Echo shook her head. "I don't think that will work. Two seconds after the seagull eats the food and flies away, it's sure to forget all about us."

"This is dumb," Spinner said. "I'm always hearing about all the crazy magic you dolphins have. And how you're always using it to help sea creatures. So why can't you use magic to send me home?"

"Our magic doesn't work that way," Echo told him.

"Then what good is it?" Spinner glared at her.

"Quit arguing," Splash said. "We need to focus. Anyway, maybe we can use our magic somehow. We could try sending a mental message to Spinner's family."

"They're probably too far away," Flip said. "We're still learning—even Echo would never be able to send a message that far without help from an adult."

"He's right," Echo agreed. "Anyway, would a shark even listen to a dolphin message?"

"Probably not," Spinner put in. He swam in a circle. "Maybe I should just charge out of here and swim as fast as I can. Sharks are faster than dolphins."

"Says who?" Flip challenged. "Dolphins are way faster!"

Splash looked frustrated. "You guys! Quit arguing!"

"Anyway, getting past the other dolphins is only part of the problem," Echo reminded the shark. "You'd still be alone out in the ocean with no idea where your family might be."

"Oh, right." Spinner glared at Flip. "But sharks are still faster."

After that, Pearl mostly stopped listening. Her friends weren't coming up with any plans that seemed as if they could work. Besides, she was focused on something else. For some reason, she couldn't stop thinking about what Bay had just said to her. She also kept remembering her talk with her father on the way to school that morning. Could something they'd said be the key to a better plan?

"This is never going to work!" Echo cried, breaking into Pearl's thoughts. "We might as well give up."

"No!" Splash said. "We can't give up. Not until Spinner is back with his family."

"Yeah." Spinner bared his teeth. "You need to help me, or else!"

"That's not very nice," Echo told him, not seeming scared of his teeth anymore. "We might want to help you more if you weren't such a . . . a . . . a *shark*!"

"I am a shark." Spinner scowled at her. "What's wrong with that?"

"I don't know." Echo sighed. "But maybe dolphins and sharks aren't meant to work together."

"I don't think that's true." Pearl spoke up.

The others all turned and looked at her. "What do you mean, Pearl?" Echo asked.

Pearl swam to the surface for a breath before answering. "I mean, I don't think it's true that dolphins and sharks can't work together," she said when she returned. "I have an idea for a way to help Spinner."

"You do?" Splash did an eager flip in the water. "What is it, Pearl?"

"This should be good," Flip told Spinner.

"Pearl's really smart. She always has good plans."

"That's right," Echo agreed. "So tell us already, Pearl!"

Pearl hesitated. "Okay," she said. "But I'm afraid you might not like it." She gulped. "Especially you, Spinner."

Spinner narrowed his eyes. "What do you mean?"

"I mean . . ." Pearl blew out a nervous stream of bubbles. "I mean, I think we should tell the teachers that you're here."

"*What?*" Spinner didn't need magic to make his voice loud. He bared his teeth. "No way. You're not telling anyone!"

Echo and Flip looked surprised. "But Pearl," Flip said. "You're the one who convinced us to keep the secret!"

"Yeah," Splash added, sounding upset. "You promised, Pearl!"

"I know." Pearl tried not to look too closely at Spinner's sharp teeth. "But I've been thinking about this a lot, and I think it's the only way to help Spinner. Just let me explain . . ."

"Are you sure about this, Pearl?" Splash asked as he and Pearl swam toward the school a few minutes later. "I mean really, really sure?"

"I think so." Pearl glanced back. They'd left Spinner behind with Echo and Flip. "Anyway, we don't have a better plan, do we?"

"I guess not." Splash sounded worried. But then he swam closer and bumped Pearl gently with his snout. "Anyway, I trust you. If you think this is the best idea, that's good enough for me."

"Thanks." Pearl hoped she wouldn't let him down. "Let's go in and see if Bay is still here."

There was no sign of the teacher inside the school cove. But after a moment, Pearl spotted the principal over by the kelp forest.

"There's Old Salty," she told Splash. "Let's talk to him."

"Okay. But I think I'm going to need more air for this," Splash said, swimming toward the surface.

Pearl did the same, gulping in a big lungful of air. Then she and Splash dove back down, heading for Old Salty. Pearl's stomach was in knots. Would her plan help Spinner? Or was she just getting him into deeper trouble?

10
So Long, Spinner

THE NEXT MORNING, PEARL ANXIOUSLY watched the school entrance from a spot just inside. "When are they going to get here?" she wondered.

"Soon, I hope." Echo shivered. "Do you think Spinner is scared?"

"If he is, he'll never admit it," Flip said. "Sharks are weird like that."

"Look," Splash cried. "Here they come!"

They all watched as Spinner swam into the cove with Old Salty swimming right next to him on one side and Riptide on the other. The rest of the students saw them, too.

"Shark!" an older student cried. "Look out, everyone!"

Wiggle darted behind a clump of coral. "Don't let him bite me!"

"Calm down, students," Bay said. She was floating nearby. "Nobody is biting anyone."

"If he tries, Riptide will stop him!" Splash's brother Finny called out. "Right, Riptide?"

"You don't have to worry," Riptide replied. "This young shark isn't here to cause trouble."

"That's right." Old Salty swam forward to address all the students. "Spinner is here so we can help him."

"Why would we do that?" Mullet called out. "Sharks are mean!"

"Spinner is no threat to us or any other dolphin," Old Salty said calmly. "He's just a lost sea creature, and as the defenders of the ocean, it's every dolphin's job to help whenever we can."

Some of the students nodded. Others still looked uncertain.

"But a shark tried to eat my grandpa once," someone said.

"I'd guess it wasn't a blacktip shark, like Spinner here," Old Salty said. "It is true that we need to be careful about some of the larger, more aggressive species. But really, most sharks aren't so different from us."

"What do you mean?" The student who called out sounded surprised. "Sharks and dolphins are nothing alike!"

Bay smiled, swimming over to join Old Salty. "Don't be so sure," she said. "Haven't you noticed how similar we look to sharks?

And of course, both our species make our homes right here in the Salty Sea."

"That's right," Pearl called out. "Sharks even go to school like us!"

"What did she say?" a dolphin near the back called out.

Echo reached over to touch Pearl's fin. "I'll help," she whispered. "Say it again."

Pearl smiled at her friend, then turned toward the others. "I said, young sharks go to school—just like us."

As she spoke, she focused her energy on making the words loud enough for the entire cove to hear. Echo's magic mingled with hers, projecting her voice successfully.

"Young Pearl is correct," Old Salty said. "We have much in common, really, as well as there being some key differences . . ."

He kept talking, describing all the ways that dolphins and sharks were similar and different. Meanwhile, Pearl looked at Spinner. He was hanging back a little behind Old Salty and the other teachers. His tail was flicking slowly from side to side, and Pearl guessed he was nervous.

I would be nervous, too, she thought. *He must feel lonely and afraid being so far away from his family and friends. He probably never even met a dolphin up close before Splash found him. And now he has to trust us to help him.*

She was glad she'd been right about the teachers. As soon as she and Splash had explained to Old Salty what had happened, the principal had offered to help Spinner get home.

"But why didn't you come to me right away?" he'd exclaimed.

"I don't know." Splash had sounded sheepish. "I guess since you're always warning us to stay away from sharks, I thought you'd be mad that we were trying to help one."

Old Salty had shaken his head. "I could never be angry with a young dolphin wanting to help another creature. That's what this school is all about, after all. I'm sorry if I didn't make that clear enough." He'd paused then, looking thoughtful. "In fact, if your new friend Spinner agrees, I'd like to use his predicament to help remind all the students of that, *hmm*?"

Spinner had agreed, but only after Pearl had told him she thought he should do it. "Okay," he'd said. "You seem pretty smart for a dolphin. If you think it's all right, I guess I'll come to your school." He'd shrugged. "I kind of want to see what it's like, anyway. Even though it's probably not as good as Shark Academy."

Now here he was, right in the middle of Coral Cove Dolphin School. And the more Old Salty talked, the friendlier the other students looked toward Spinner.

"This is great," Splash whispered, nudging Pearl with his fin. "After this, I bet everyone will think about sharks differently."

Flip heard him and floated closer. "Yeah, blacktips maybe," he said. "But I'm still going to swim away if I see a tiger shark coming at me in Bigsky Basin!"

Several minutes later, Old Salty was still talking. Somehow, he'd gotten distracted from the topic of sharks and had moved on to one of his favorite subjects: algae. Most of the other dolphins looked bored, and Spinner looked confused.

Luckily, just then several adult dolphins swam into the school. Pearl spotted her father among them. Echo's mother was there, too.

"Good news," Echo's mother said, swimming forward to talk to the teachers. "I was able to locate Spinner's family."

"Excellent!" Old Salty beamed at her, not seeming to mind being interrupted.

"Yay, Echo's mom!" Flip cheered.

Pearl smiled. Echo's mother had even stronger magic than most dolphins. Old Salty had asked her to use mental messaging to try to locate Spinner's family.

"You found them?" Spinner exclaimed, swimming over to Echo's mother.

"Yes, young one." She smiled at him. "We can take you home now."

"Hooray!" Splash yelled, doing three quick flips underwater, then dashing toward the shark. "We did it, Spinner!"

"Yeah!" Spinner yelled. He crashed into Splash with his snout.

Then both of them zipped up, leaping up and out of the water and doing that unusual spin in the air before splashing down again.

Pearl laughed. "Come on," she told Echo and Flip. "Let's see if they'll let us swim along."

"They'd better." Echo led the way toward the adults. "Mom promised I could come. She says it will be good for me to see a new part of the Salty Sea."

Sure enough, the friends were welcomed by the adults. Old Salty and a few other teachers were staying behind with the other students, though Bay and Riptide were going with Spinner.

"Ready to go, Pearl?" her father asked, stroking her head with his fin.

"I'm ready." Pearl smiled at the young shark. "Are you ready, Spinner?"

"What do you think?" Spinner said, baring his teeth at her. But this time, Pearl could tell right away that he was smiling.

As the group swam toward the exit, Pearl noticed Mullet racing to catch up. "Hey, wait," he called.

Pearl gulped. In all the excitement, she'd almost forgotten about Mullet. Was he about to tell everyone how Spinner had chased him? If so, would that change the other dolphins' minds about helping Spinner get home?

"Yes? What is it, Mullet?" Bay asked.

Mullet stopped in front of her, shooting a sidelong look toward Spinner. "It's just—um, can I come, too?" Mullet blurted out. "I mean, you're letting these first years swim along, right? I could help keep an eye on them. You know, stay with them so they don't get scared when they see the sharks."

"What?" Flip exclaimed. "Are you—"

But Pearl nudged him. "*Shh*," she whispered. "Don't say it."

Splash snorted. Pearl thought he might laugh, so she nudged him, too.

"My dad says to *Always Choose Kindness*," she reminded him quietly.

Splash seemed to understand. Ignoring Mullet as he joined the group, Splash swam to Spinner's side.

"Come on, friend," he said, touching the shark's fin with his own. "Let's get you home."

Read on for a sneak

peek at the next

Dolphin
School

story!

Flip's
Surprise Talent

"Show Off Day?" Flip exclaimed. "Wow, that's awesome!"

"Yeah!" Splash did three flips in a row. "I can't believe it's here already—I can't wait!"

Echo laughed. "This is the best day ever!"

Pearl looked around. Everyone else seemed just as excited as her friends. They were chattering and doing flips and blowing bubbles. Old Salty just watched and smiled.

"Show Off Day?" Pearl said to her friends. "What's that?"

"Are you joking?" Flip said. "Everyone knows what Show Off Day is."

"I don't," Pearl said.

"It's when all the students at Coral Cove Dolphin School get to show off what they've learned so far that year," Echo explained. "The whole dolphin community comes to watch."

Splash nodded. "I thought everyone went. Didn't you ever go with your pod?"

One of the teachers swam over. Her name was Bay, and she taught Pearl's two favorite classes, Magic and Music.

"I heard what you were saying," she told the young dolphins. "There's a good reason why Pearl hasn't been to Show Off Day before. As you all know, her pod has a very important job protecting baby sea turtles."

Pearl nodded. Lots of turtles laid their eggs on the island by her pod's lagoon. The dolphins helped guide the hatchlings out to sea where they would be safe from hungry gulls and other land predators.

"Yeah, we know all about that," Flip said.

"What do a bunch of baby turtles have to do with Show Off Day?"

"Normally Show Off Day happens around the same time of year that the turtles hatch," Bay explained. "That's why Pearl's pod never came before. They didn't want to leave their lagoon during that very important time."

"Oh." Pearl was worried. "Does that mean I'll have to miss Show Off Day this year, too?"

Bay smiled. "No, you'll be there, and so will your pod," she assured Pearl. "We made it earlier this year so you won't have to miss it."

"Really?" Echo bumped Pearl's side with her snout. "That's super, Pearl!"

"Yeah," Splash said. "Show Off Day wouldn't be the same without you."

Flip nodded. "It's great! Everyone talks about the best performances all year afterward.

This year, one of those best performances is going to be me!"

Bay chuckled. "All we ask is that you do your best, Flip. And have fun, of course."

Pearl smiled at Bay. "Thanks for telling me about Show Off Day," she said. "Now I can't wait to be a part of it."

Just then Old Salty called for attention again. "I'm glad you're all so excited," he told all the students with a chuckle. "We'll have our regular classes today as usual. But tomorrow you'll have the whole day to figure out your routines and get started on practicing. Show Off Day will be two days after that."

"That's right." Bay swam forward to join him. "As always, group performances are encouraged. Remember that dolphins are at their best when they work together."

Pearl looked at her friends. "Group performances?"

"Yeah!" Splash did a flip. "Let's work together, okay?"

"Sure," Echo said. "We make a good group."

Flip zipped up to get a breath of air, then swam back down. "So what kind of performance should we do?" he asked. "Whatever it is, it has to be great—I want our group to be the best!"

"We will be," Pearl said with a smile. "Because we're compatible. That's what Shelly said, remember?"

Echo didn't seem to be listening. She was staring off into the distance with a thoughtful expression.

"Echo?" Pearl said. "What are you thinking about?"

Echo smiled and sent out a burst of sparkly magic lights. "I was just thinking about how we could do a super amazing magic display," she said eagerly. "I already have some ideas for really fancy stuff we could do."

"A magic display?" Splash sounded dubious. "Everyone will be doing that kind of thing. I think we should do a cool jumping and swimming routine instead."

Pearl didn't like the sound of that. She wasn't very good at jumping and swimming. This would be her first Show Off Day ever, and she wanted their performance to be something she could do well. Something like magic, or . . .

"What about singing a song?" she blurted out, realizing it was the perfect idea. "We've been learning some neat things in Music class."

Flip looked over as Old Salty called out for everyone to swim to their first classes. "Like I said, I don't care what we do," he said. "I'm great at everything. And I can't wait to show it off!"

The Rescue Princesses

These are no ordinary princesses—
they're Rescue Princesses!

Puppy Powers

Secret Kingdom

Be in on the secret.
Collect them all!

Enjoy six sparkling adventures.

RAINBOW magic™

Which Magical Fairies Have You Met?

- ❏ The Rainbow Fairies
- ❏ The Weather Fairies
- ❏ The Jewel Fairies
- ❏ The Pet Fairies
- ❏ The Dance Fairies
- ❏ The Music Fairies
- ❏ The Sports Fairies
- ❏ The Party Fairies
- ❏ The Ocean Fairies
- ❏ The Night Fairies
- ❏ The Magical Animal Fairies
- ❏ The Princess Fairies
- ❏ The Superstar Fairies
- ❏ The Fashion Fairies
- ❏ The Sugar & Spice Fairies
- ❏ The Earth Fairies
- ❏ The Magical Crafts Fairies
- ❏ The Baby Animal Rescue Fairies

■SCHOLASTIC

Find all of your favorite fairy friends at
scholastic.com/rainbowmagic

RMFAIRY